Ethan Shadows

Whispers of the Forgotten

Whispers of the Forgotten

by

Ethan Shadows

Ethan Shadows

To all my teachers who have inspired me:

Your wisdom and guidance have been the compass leading me through the darkest woods and the brightest days. You ignited the flames of curiosity and courage within me, teaching me to face the unknown with both skepticism and wonder. Your unwavering belief in my potential gave me the strength to pursue my dreams, even when the path seemed impossible.

This book is a testament to your lessons, a tribute to your patience, and a reflection of the profound impact you've had on my life. I am forever grateful for your inspiration and the light you've shared with me.

Thank you, from the depths of my heart.

.

Whispers of the Forgotten

Ethan Shadows

Table of Contents

Prologue

The old house at the end of Elm Street had always held a mysterious aura. The townsfolk whispered about it, claiming it was haunted. To Daniel Miller, it was his grandfather's home, filled with memories of love and laughter. When his grandfather passed away, Daniel inherited not just the house but a chilling legacy – the ability to communicate with ghosts.

On a crisp autumn evening, Daniel stood at the edge of the overgrown lawn, staring at the imposing structure. The house seemed to breathe, its wooden boards creaking under the weight of time. Ivy clung to the walls, and the windows, clouded with dust, reflected the setting sun. The air was thick with the scent of decaying leaves and damp earth.

Daniel's mother, Anna, stood beside him, her eyes glistening with tears. "Your grandfather loved this house," she said softly. "He believed it held secrets."

Secrets. The word hung in the air like a whisper. Daniel shivered, pulling his jacket tighter around him. "Let's go inside," he said, his voice barely audible.

The front door creaked open, revealing a dimly lit foyer. Dust motes danced in the air, illuminated by the fading sunlight streaming through the windows. Daniel's gaze was drawn to the old grandfather clock in the corner, its pendulum swinging slowly, marking the passage of time.

Anna placed a hand on Daniel's shoulder. "Take your time, sweetheart. I'll be in the kitchen if you need me."

Daniel nodded, his eyes lingering on the staircase leading to the second floor. He had always been curious about his grandfather's study, a room he had never been allowed to enter. Today, that would change.

With hesitant steps, Daniel made his way up the stairs. Each step creaked under his weight, echoing through the silent house. At the end of the hallway, he found the door to the study slightly ajar. Pushing it open, he stepped inside.

The study was a time capsule, untouched by the years. Shelves lined with books covered every wall, and the air was thick with the scent of aged paper and leather. In the center of the room stood an oak desk, cluttered with papers, quills, and an old inkpot. On the desk lay a tattered journal, its pages yellowed with age.

Daniel approached the desk, his heart pounding. The journal was open, revealing his grandfather's meticulous handwriting. He hesitated for a moment before picking it up.

"Daniel, if you're reading this, it means I've passed on. You have inherited a gift, a curse. You can see and speak with the souls that linger between this world and the next."

Daniel's hands trembled as he read the words. His grandfather had always been a mysterious figure, full of strange stories and cryptic advice. But this – this was something entirely different.

"I discovered this ability when I was your age," the journal continued. "It can be both a blessing and a burden. You must learn to navigate the world of the spirits, to help those who are lost find their way. But be warned, not all spirits are benevolent."

A chill ran down Daniel's spine. He closed the journal, his mind racing. Could it be true? Could he really communicate with ghosts?

As if in response to his thoughts, a cold breeze swept through the room, ruffling the pages of the journal. Daniel looked around, his heart pounding in his chest. The room seemed to darken, the shadows growing longer and deeper.

"Hello?" he called out, his voice trembling.

For a moment, there was only silence. Then, faintly, he heard a whisper.

"Daniel..."

He spun around, searching for the source of the voice. The room was empty, yet he felt a presence, a weight pressing down on him.

"Who are you?" he asked, his voice barely above a whisper.

There was no response. The air grew colder, and Daniel could see his breath in the dim light. He took a step back, his heart racing.

And then, as quickly as it had come, the presence was gone. The room warmed, the shadows receded, and the only sound was the steady ticking of the grandfather clock downstairs.

Daniel stood in the center of the study, his mind reeling. His grandfather's words echoed in his head. He had inherited a gift – a curse. He could communicate with ghosts.

And so, the journey began.

Ethan Shadows

Chapter 1
<u>The Inheritance</u>

The following days passed in a blur. Daniel and his mother spent hours cleaning the old house, sorting through his grandfather's belongings. Each room held memories; echoes of a life once lived. But for Daniel, the study was the heart of the house, the place where his grandfather's secrets were kept.

One evening, after his mother had gone to bed, Daniel returned to the study. He sat at the desk; the journal open before him. He read through the entries, learning about his grandfather's encounters with the spirit world.

"I first saw them when I was twelve," one entry read. "They came to me in the night, seeking help. It was terrifying at first, but

Whispers of the Forgotten

over time, I learned to listen, to understand their pain. I helped them find peace."

Daniel felt a strange connection to his grandfather, a bond that transcended time and death. He wanted to learn, to understand this gift – this curse. But he was also afraid. What if he couldn't handle it? What if the spirits were too much for him?

His thoughts were interrupted by a faint sound, a whisper. He looked up, his heart pounding. The room seemed to darken, the air growing cold.

"Daniel..." the voice called again.

He stood up, his hands trembling. "Who's there?"

The shadows in the corner of the room seemed to shift, forming a shape – a young girl, no older than eight, with sad, hollow eyes. She was translucent, her form flickering like a candle flame.

"Help me," she whispered, her voice echoing in the silence.

Daniel stumbled back, his heart racing. "Who are you?"

"Emily," she replied. "I'm lost. Please, help me find my way."

Daniel took a deep breath, trying to steady himself. "How can I help you?"

Emily's eyes filled with tears. "I don't know. I've been lost for so long. I can't find my way home."

Daniel felt a pang of sympathy for the girl. He wanted to help her, but he didn't know how. "I'll try," he said softly. "I'll try to help you."

Emily smiled faintly, her form flickering. "Thank you," she whispered before fading away.

Daniel sat back down, his mind racing. He had seen his first ghost, and she needed his help. He knew it was just the beginning. There would be more spirits, more lost souls seeking his guidance.

And he was determined to help them.

The next morning, Daniel woke early, his mind still buzzing from the encounter with Emily. He had so many questions, so many uncertainties. But he knew he couldn't face them alone.

At breakfast, he tried to bring it up with his mother. "Mom, did Grandpa ever talk to you about... ghosts?"

Anna looked up from her coffee, her expression thoughtful. "Your grandfather had many stories. He believed in things most people don't understand. Why do you ask?"

Daniel hesitated. "I just... I found his journal. It talks about seeing and helping spirits."

Anna sighed, setting her cup down. "Your grandfather was a special man, Daniel. He saw the world differently. If you're reading his journal, you should take it seriously. But also remember, not everything is as it seems."

Daniel nodded, though his mind was still filled with doubt. He knew he had to explore this gift – this curse – on his own.

That afternoon, while cleaning out the attic, Daniel found a small box labeled "For Daniel." Inside were various trinkets and mementos from his grandfather's life, including an old key and a letter.

"My dear Daniel," the letter began. "This key opens a special drawer in my desk. Inside, you'll find tools that will help you navigate your new reality. Use them wisely."

Daniel's curiosity was piqued. He returned to the study and found the hidden drawer. Inside were various items: a pocket watch, a set of old coins, a compass, and a small crystal. Each item seemed to hum with energy.

That evening, as Daniel sat in the study, he felt a presence again. This time, it was stronger, more insistent. He looked up to see a figure standing in the corner – an elderly man with kind eyes.

"Grandpa?" Daniel whispered.

The figure nodded; his eyes filled with warmth. "Daniel, you have a great responsibility. The tools in the drawer will help you understand the spirits and their needs. Trust your instincts."

Daniel felt a wave of reassurance. "Thank you, Grandpa. I'll do my best."

The figure smiled before fading away. Daniel knew he had a long journey ahead, but he was ready to face it.

Chapter 2
<u>The First Encounter</u>

The next morning, Daniel woke early, his mind still buzzing from the encounter with Emily and the visit from his grandfather's spirit. He had so many questions, so many uncertainties. But he knew he couldn't face them alone.

At breakfast, he tried to bring it up with his mother. "Mom, did Grandpa ever talk to you about... ghosts?"

Anna looked up from her coffee, her expression thoughtful. "Your grandfather had many stories. He believed in things most people don't understand. Why do you ask?"

Daniel hesitated. "I just... I found his journal. It talks about seeing and helping spirits."

Whispers of the Forgotten

Anna sighed, setting her cup down. "Your grandfather was a special man, Daniel. He saw the world differently. If you're reading his journal, you should take it seriously. But also remember, not everything is as it seems."

Daniel nodded, though his mind was still filled with doubt. He knew he had to explore this gift – this curse – on his own.

At school, Daniel tried to focus on his classes, but his thoughts kept drifting back to Emily and his grandfather's journal. During lunch, he met up with Lily, his best friend. They sat under their usual tree in the schoolyard, the autumn leaves crunching beneath them.

"You look distracted," Lily said, biting into her sandwich. "What's up?"

Daniel took a deep breath. "I need to tell you something, but you have to promise not to think I'm crazy."

Lily raised an eyebrow. "Okay, I promise. What's going on?"

Daniel explained everything – his grandfather's journal, the ability to see ghosts, and his encounter with Emily. As he spoke, Lily's expression shifted from skepticism to concern.

"Wow," she said when he finished. "That's... a lot to take in."

"I know," Daniel replied. "I don't know what to do. How can I help these spirits?"

Lily thought for a moment. "Maybe we can figure it out together. Two heads are better than one, right?"

Daniel felt a wave of relief. "Thanks, Lily. I really appreciate it."

Lily smiled. "We'll start with Emily. Maybe we can find out more about her and why she's lost."

That evening, Daniel and Lily met at the library, determined to learn more about Emily. They searched through old newspapers and archives, looking for any mention of a girl named Emily who had gone missing or died.

Hours passed, and just as they were about to give up, Lily found an article from ten years ago. "Daniel, look at this."

Daniel leaned over, reading the headline: "Local Girl Missing – Search Continues." The article described a young girl named Emily who had disappeared without a trace.

"That's her," Daniel said, his voice trembling. "She must be the ghost I saw."

Lily nodded. "But why is she still here? What happened to her?"

Daniel shook his head. "I don't know, but we need to find out. Maybe if we learn more about her, we can help her move on."

That night, Daniel returned to his grandfather's study. He opened the journal, hoping to find guidance. As he read, he felt a cold breeze, and Emily appeared once again.

"Emily," he said softly. "I found an article about you. You went missing ten years ago."

Emily's eyes filled with tears. "I remember... I was playing near the river. I fell in, and everything went dark. When I woke up, I was here, and I couldn't find my way home."

Daniel's heart ached for her. "I'm so sorry, Emily. We'll help you. We'll find a way to bring you peace."

Emily smiled faintly. "Thank you, Daniel. You're very kind."

As Emily faded away, Daniel felt a renewed sense of purpose. He would help Emily, and any other spirits who came to him. It was his duty, his legacy.

The next day, Daniel confided in Ethan, his childhood friend who was skeptical of the supernatural but loyal. Ethan listened intently; his brow furrowed with concern.

"Daniel, are you sure about this? It sounds... crazy," Ethan said, his voice tinged with worry.

"I know it does," Daniel replied. "But I need you to believe me. I need your help."

Ethan sighed, running a hand through his hair. "Alright, I'll help. But we need to be careful."

With Ethan on board, Daniel felt a renewed sense of determination. They decided to visit Mrs. Thompson, the neighbor who knew a lot about the history of the house and the town's ghost stories.

Mrs. Thompson welcomed them into her home, her eyes twinkling with curiosity. "What brings you boys here today?"

Daniel explained everything – his grandfather's journal, the encounters with ghosts, and their quest to help Emily.

Mrs. Thompson nodded thoughtfully. "Your grandfather was a wise man, Daniel. He knew the spirits well. The house has a long history, filled with both light and darkness. If you truly wish to help Emily, you must understand the balance between the two."

She shared stories of her own encounters with spirits and offered advice on how to navigate the supernatural world. Daniel felt a sense of reassurance knowing he had allies in his journey.

That night, Daniel sat in the study, reflecting on the events of the past few days. He knew his path wouldn't be easy, but he was ready to face whatever challenges lay ahead.

Chapter 3
<u>Whispers in the Night</u>

That evening, Daniel and Lily met at the library, determined to learn more about Emily. They searched through old newspapers and archives, looking for any mention of a girl named Emily who had gone missing or died.

Hours passed, and just as they were about to give up, Lily found an article from ten years ago. "Daniel, look at this."

Daniel leaned over, reading the headline: "Local Girl Missing – Search Continues." The article described a young girl named Emily who had disappeared without a trace.

"That's her," Daniel said, his voice trembling. "She must be the ghost I saw."

Whispers of the Forgotten

Lily nodded. "But why is she still here? What happened to her?"

Daniel shook his head. "I don't know, but we need to find out. Maybe if we learn more about her, we can help her move on."

They continued their research, diving into more articles and records. They found several reports about the river where Emily had gone missing. It was a popular spot for children to play, but it had also been the site of numerous accidents and tragedies over the years.

As they dug deeper, they discovered a chilling pattern – every ten years, a child had gone missing near the river, their bodies never found. It seemed Emily was just one of many.

The realization sent a shiver down Daniel's spine. "There's something wrong with that place," he said, his voice barely above a whisper. "We need to find out what's causing these disappearances."

That night, Daniel returned to his grandfather's study. He opened the journal, hoping to find guidance. As he read, he felt a cold breeze, and Emily appeared once again.

"Emily," he said softly. "I found an article about you. You went missing ten years ago."

Emily's eyes filled with tears. "I remember... I was playing near the river. I fell in, and everything went dark. When I woke up, I was here, and I couldn't find my way home."

Daniel's heart ached for her. "I'm so sorry, Emily. We'll help you. We'll find a way to bring you peace."

Emily smiled faintly. "Thank you, Daniel. You're very kind."

As Emily faded away, Daniel felt a renewed sense of purpose. He would help Emily, and any other spirits who came to him. It was his duty, his legacy.

The next day, Daniel confided in Ethan, his childhood friend who was skeptical of the supernatural but loyal. Ethan listened intently; his brow furrowed with concern.

"Daniel, are you sure about this? It sounds... crazy," Ethan said, his voice tinged with worry.

"I know it does," Daniel replied. "But I need you to believe me. I need your help."

Ethan sighed, running a hand through his hair. "Alright, I'll help. But we need to be careful."

With Ethan on board, Daniel felt a renewed sense of determination. They decided to visit Mrs. Thompson, the neighbor who knew a lot about the history of the house and the town's ghost stories.

Mrs. Thompson welcomed them into her home, her eyes twinkling with curiosity. "What brings you boys here today?"

Daniel explained everything – his grandfather's journal, the encounters with ghosts, and their quest to help Emily.

Mrs. Thompson nodded thoughtfully. "Your grandfather was a wise man, Daniel. He knew the spirits well. The house has a long history, filled with both light and darkness. If you truly wish to help Emily, you must understand the balance between the two."

She shared stories of her own encounters with spirits and offered advice on how to navigate the supernatural world. Daniel felt a sense of reassurance knowing he had allies in his journey.

That night, Daniel sat in the study, reflecting on the events of the past few days. He knew his path wouldn't be easy, but he was ready to face whatever challenges lay ahead.

Chapter 4
<u>The Visions</u>

The first vision came in the middle of the night. Daniel was jolted awake, his heart pounding. He saw flashes of chaos – a school hallway, screams, blood. And then, a face – a boy from his school, holding a gun.

The vision ended as abruptly as it began, leaving Daniel drenched in sweat. He sat up in bed, his heart racing. What was that? Was it a warning? A premonition?

The next day at school, Daniel couldn't shake the images from his mind. He tried to identify the boy from his vision, scanning the faces of his classmates. He saw him in the cafeteria – a quiet, withdrawn boy named Jason. Daniel didn't know much about him, but he knew he had to find a way to stop what he had seen.

Whispers of the Forgotten

During lunch, Daniel told Lily about the vision. "I think it's going to happen soon. We have to do something."

Lily looked worried. "But what can we do? We can't just accuse him without any proof."

"I know," Daniel replied, feeling helpless. "But we can't just ignore it either."

They decided to keep an eye on Jason, to look for any signs that he might be planning something. Daniel also consulted the ghosts, hoping they could provide more information.

That night, Emily appeared again, her expression serious. "The vision you saw – it's real. You must stop it."

"But how?" Daniel asked, his voice breaking. "I don't know what to do."

"Trust the spirits," Emily said. "They will guide you."

The next day, Daniel approached Jason in the hallway, trying to strike up a conversation. Jason seemed distant, his eyes filled with a mix of anger and sadness.

"Hey, Jason," Daniel said, forcing a smile. "How's it going?"

Jason glanced at him; his expression guarded. "Fine," he muttered before walking away.

Daniel watched him go, a knot of worry tightening in his chest. He knew he needed to find a way to get through to Jason, to understand what was driving him to such a dark place.

During lunch, Daniel and Lily observed Jason from a distance. They noticed him spending time with a group of older kids, who seemed to be influencing his behavior. Daniel's sense of urgency grew.

That evening, Daniel sought guidance from the spirits. Emily appeared, along with a new spirit – a stern-looking man with piercing eyes.

"Who are you?" Daniel asked, his voice trembling.

"I am Samuel," the spirit replied. "I was a teacher at your school many years ago. I have seen many troubled souls like Jason. You must reach him before it's too late."

Daniel nodded, his determination solidifying. "I'll do whatever it takes."

Samuel and Emily provided Daniel with more details about Jason's struggles and the influences around him. With this knowledge, Daniel devised a plan to intervene.

The next day, Daniel and Lily approached Jason again, offering him kindness and understanding. They invited him to join them for lunch, hoping to break through his walls.

At first, Jason was hesitant, but as the days passed, he began to open up. He shared bits and pieces of his life – the bullying, the loneliness, the anger that had been festering inside him.

Daniel listened intently, his heart aching for Jason. He knew he had to find a way to help him see that violence wasn't the answer.

One evening, as Daniel sat in his room, Emily and Samuel appeared once more. "You are making progress, Daniel," Samuel said. "But the danger is still imminent. You must act quickly."

Daniel felt a surge of determination. "I will," he vowed. "I won't let this happen."

With the spirits' guidance, Daniel continued to reach out to Jason, showing him that there were people who cared about him, who wanted to help him find a better path.

Chapter 5
Warnings and Doubts

As the days passed, Daniel's anxiety grew. He knew the vision was drawing closer, and he felt a growing sense of urgency. He tried to warn the school authorities, including his mother, the principal, but his pleas fell on deaf ears.

"Daniel, I understand you're scared," his mother said gently. "But we can't act on visions. We need real evidence."

Daniel felt frustrated and helpless. He knew he was running out of time. He turned to the ghosts for guidance, hoping they could help him find a way to prevent the tragedy.

One night, as Daniel sat in his room, Emily appeared again, her eyes wide with urgency. "The shooting," she whispered. "It's going to happen soon. You must stop it."

Whispers of the Forgotten

"But how?" Daniel asked, his voice trembling.

"Trust the spirits," Emily said. "They will guide you."

With Emily's reassurance, Daniel felt a renewed sense of determination. He continued to reach out to Jason, hoping to find a way to change his mind.

During lunch, Daniel and Lily noticed Jason growing more withdrawn and agitated. They decided to confront him, hoping to understand what was driving him to such a dark place.

"Jason, we care about you," Daniel said, his voice filled with sincerity. "Please, talk to us."

Jason's eyes filled with tears. "You don't understand," he muttered. "You can't help me."

Daniel's heart ached for him. "We can try," he said softly. "You don't have to go through this alone."

Jason looked at them, his expression torn. "Maybe... maybe you're right," he whispered.

That evening, Daniel and Lily met with Ethan, hoping to enlist his help. Ethan listened intently, his skepticism slowly giving way to concern.

"Alright," Ethan said, his voice steady. "I'm in. Let's figure this out together."

With Ethan on board, they devised a plan to keep an eye on Jason and intervene if necessary. They knew the stakes were high, and they couldn't afford to make any mistakes.

Daniel sought guidance from the spirits, who provided more details about Jason's plans and the layout of the school. With each vision, Daniel's resolve grew stronger.

As the day of the shooting approached, Daniel and his friends grew more anxious. They double-checked their plans, ensuring everything was in place. The ghosts continued to provide guidance, their whispers growing more urgent.

Daniel tried one last time to warn his mother. "Mom, please, you have to believe me. Something terrible is going to happen."

Anna looked at him, her expression pained. "Daniel, I love you, but I can't take action based on visions. Please, try to stay calm."

Daniel felt a surge of frustration, but he knew he couldn't give up. He and Lily had to act, with or without help from the authorities.

With the spirits' guidance, Daniel and his friends positioned themselves strategically around the school, ready to act at a moment's notice. The air was thick with tension, each second dragging on like an eternity.

Chapter 6
The Unseen Allies

The ghosts began to show Daniel more – the shooter's plans, the layout of the school, the timing. With each vision, Daniel's resolve grew stronger. He had to prevent this tragedy, even if no one believed him.

Daniel and Lily devised a plan. They mapped out the school, identifying key areas where they could intervene. The ghosts provided crucial details, helping them piece together the shooter's movements.

"We'll need to be in position before he arrives," Daniel said, his voice steady. "We can't afford to make any mistakes."

Lily nodded. "We'll do whatever it takes."

Whispers of the Forgotten

Ethan Shadows

That evening, they met at the old house, going over their plan in detail. Ethan joined them, his skepticism replaced by a sense of duty.

"We have to stop this," Ethan said, his voice firm. "We can't let it happen."

Daniel felt a surge of gratitude for his friends. They were in this together, and he knew they would do whatever it took to prevent the tragedy.

The ghosts continued to provide guidance; their whispers more urgent than ever. Daniel felt a strange sense of connection with them, as if they were all working towards a common goal.

One night, as Daniel sat in his room, he felt a cold breeze and saw a figure standing in the corner. It was a woman, her eyes filled with sorrow.

Whispers of the Forgotten

"Who are you?" Daniel asked, his voice trembling.

"I am Sarah," the woman replied. "I was a victim of violence many years ago. I have come to help you."

Daniel felt a wave of compassion for her. "Thank you, Sarah. We need all the help we can get."

Sarah nodded. "I will guide you. You must trust your instincts and act quickly."

With Sarah's guidance, Daniel felt a renewed sense of determination. He and his friends continued to refine their plan, ensuring they were ready for whatever might happen.

As the day of the shooting approached, Daniel and his friends grew more anxious. They double-checked their plans, ensuring everything was in place. The ghosts continued to provide guidance, their whispers growing more urgent.

Daniel tried one last time to warn his mother. "Mom, please, you have to believe me. Something terrible is going to happen."

Anna looked at him, her expression pained. "Daniel, I love you, but I can't take action based on visions. Please, try to stay calm."

Daniel felt a surge of frustration, but he knew he couldn't give up. He and Lily had to act, with or without help from the authorities.

With the spirits' guidance, Daniel and his friends positioned themselves strategically around the school, ready to act at a moment's notice. The air was thick with tension, each second dragging on like an eternity.

Chapter 7
<u>The Warning</u>

As the day of the shooting approached, Daniel and Lily grew more anxious. They double-checked their plans, ensuring everything was in place. The ghosts continued to provide guidance, their whispers growing more urgent.

Daniel tried one last time to warn his mother. "Mom, please, you have to believe me. Something terrible is going to happen."

Anna looked at him, her expression pained. "Daniel, I love you, but I can't take action based on visions. Please, try to stay calm."

Daniel felt a surge of frustration, but he knew he couldn't give up. He and Lily had to act, with or without help from the authorities.

Ethan Shadows

With the spirits' guidance, Daniel and his friends positioned themselves strategically around the school, ready to act at a moment's notice. The air was thick with tension, each second dragging on like an eternity.

Daniel felt a chill run down his spine as he watched the students milling about, unaware of the danger. He knew he couldn't let them down.

The ghosts whispered in his ear, guiding him. "Stay strong, Daniel. You can do this."

That morning, Daniel and Lily arrived at school early. They took their positions, keeping a watchful eye on Jason and the other students. The tension was palpable, the air thick with anticipation.

As the lunch bell rang, signaling the end of the period, Daniel saw Jason approaching the entrance. His heart raced as he noticed the bulge under Jason's jacket – the gun.

Whispers of the Forgotten

"Now," Daniel whispered to Lily.

They stepped forward, blocking Jason's path. "Jason, wait," Daniel said, his voice shaking.

Jason looked startled; his eyes wide with fear. "What are you doing? Get out of my way."

"We know what you're planning," Daniel said, trying to keep his voice steady. "You don't have to do this."

Jason's hand moved towards his jacket, but Daniel reached out, grabbing his arm. "Please, Jason. There's another way."

For a moment, Jason hesitated. The hallway seemed to freeze; the air thick with tension. The ghosts whispered in Daniel's ear, urging him on.

"Listen to me," Daniel said, his voice filled with urgency. "We care about you. We want to help you."

Jason's eyes filled with tears. "You don't understand," he muttered. "I'm lost."

Daniel's heart ached for him. "We can help you find your way," he said softly. "You don't have to do this."

Jason looked at him, his expression torn. "Maybe... maybe you're right," he whispered.

Before Jason could make a move, the police arrived, apprehending him and securing the school. The threat was over, but the emotional toll lingered.

Daniel felt a wave of relief and exhaustion. He had done what he set out to do, but the weight of the experience weighed heavily on him.

Chapter 8
<u>The Plan</u>

On the day of the shooting, Daniel and Lily arrived at school early. They positioned themselves strategically, ready to act. The air was thick with tension, each second dragging on like an eternity.

Daniel felt a chill run down his spine as he watched the students milling about, unaware of the danger. He knew he couldn't let them down.

The ghosts whispered in his ear, guiding him. "Stay strong, Daniel. You can do this."

That morning, Daniel and Lily arrived at school early. They took their positions, keeping a watchful eye on Jason and the other students. The tension was palpable, the air thick with anticipation.

Whispers of the Forgotten

Ethan Shadows

As the lunch bell rang, signaling the end of the period, Daniel saw Jason approaching the entrance. His heart raced as he noticed the bulge under Jason's jacket – the gun.

"Now," Daniel whispered to Lily.

They stepped forward, blocking Jason's path. "Jason, wait," Daniel said, his voice shaking.

Jason looked startled; his eyes wide with fear. "What are you doing? Get out of my way."

"We know what you're planning," Daniel said, trying to keep his voice steady. "You don't have to do this."

Jason's hand moved towards his jacket, but Daniel reached out, grabbing his arm. "Please, Jason. There's another way."

For a moment, Jason hesitated. The hallway seemed to freeze; the air thick with tension.

Ethan Shadows

The ghosts whispered in Daniel's ear, urging him on.

"Listen to me," Daniel said, his voice filled with urgency. "We care about you. We want to help you."

Jason's eyes filled with tears. "You don't understand," he muttered. "I'm lost."

Daniel's heart ached for him. "We can help you find your way," he said softly. "You don't have to do this."

Jason looked at him, his expression torn. "Maybe... maybe you're right," he whispered.

Before Jason could make a move, the police arrived, apprehending him and securing the school. The threat was over, but the emotional toll lingered.

Daniel felt a wave of relief and exhaustion. He had done what he set out to do, but the

Whispers of the Forgotten

weight of the experience weighed heavily on him.

Chapter 9
The Day of Reckoning

The school day began like any other, but Daniel's heart was pounding in his chest. He kept a close eye on Jason, watching for any signs of trouble. As the day progressed, the tension grew unbearable.

During lunch, Daniel and Lily took their positions near the main entrance. They knew this was where Jason would make his move. Daniel's hands trembled as he clutched his phone, ready to call for help.

The school day began like any other, but Daniel's heart was pounding in his chest. He kept a close eye on Jason, watching for any signs of trouble. As the day progressed, the tension grew unbearable.

During lunch, Daniel and Lily took their positions near the main entrance. They knew

Whispers of the Forgotten

this was where Jason would make his move. Daniel's hands trembled as he clutched his phone, ready to call for help.

As the lunch bell rang, signaling the end of the period, Daniel saw Jason approaching the entrance. His heart raced as he noticed the bulge under Jason's jacket – the gun.

"Now," Daniel whispered to Lily.

They stepped forward, blocking Jason's path. "Jason, wait," Daniel said, his voice shaking.

Jason looked startled; his eyes wide with fear. "What are you doing? Get out of my way."

"We know what you're planning," Daniel said, trying to keep his voice steady. "You don't have to do this."

Jason's hand moved towards his jacket, but Daniel reached out, grabbing his arm. "Please, Jason. There's another way."

Ethan Shadows

For a moment, Jason hesitated. The hallway seemed to freeze; the air thick with tension. The ghosts whispered in Daniel's ear, urging him on.

"Listen to me," Daniel said, his voice filled with urgency. "We care about you. We want to help you."

Jason's eyes filled with tears. "You don't understand," he muttered. "I'm lost."

Daniel's heart ached for him. "We can help you find your way," he said softly. "You don't have to do this."

Jason looked at him, his expression torn. "Maybe... maybe you're right," he whispered.

Before Jason could make a move, the police arrived, apprehending him and securing the school. The threat was over, but the emotional toll lingered.

Whispers of the Forgotten

Daniel felt a wave of relief and exhaustion. He had done what he set out to do, but the weight of the experience weighed heavily on him.

Chapter 10
The Confrontation

As the lunch bell rang, signaling the end of the period, Daniel saw Jason approaching the entrance. His heart raced as he noticed the bulge under Jason's jacket – the gun.

"Now," Daniel whispered to Lily.

They stepped forward, blocking Jason's path. "Jason, wait," Daniel said, his voice shaking.

Jason looked startled; his eyes wide with fear. "What are you doing? Get out of my way."

"We know what you're planning," Daniel said, trying to keep his voice steady. "You don't have to do this."

Jason's hand moved towards his jacket, but Daniel reached out, grabbing his arm. "Please, Jason. There's another way."

For a moment, Jason hesitated. The hallway seemed to freeze; the air thick with tension. The ghosts whispered in Daniel's ear, urging him on.

"Listen to me," Daniel said, his voice filled with urgency. "We care about you. We want to help you."

Jason's eyes filled with tears. "You don't understand," he muttered. "I'm lost."

Daniel's heart ached for him. "We can help you find your way," he said softly. "You don't have to do this."

Jason looked at him, his expression torn. "Maybe... maybe you're right," he whispered.

Before Jason could make a move, the police arrived, apprehending him and securing the school. The threat was over, but the emotional toll lingered.

Daniel felt a wave of relief and exhaustion. He had done what he set out to do, but the weight of the experience weighed heavily on him.

Chapter 11
The Aftermath

The police arrived just in time, apprehending Jason before he could carry out his plan. The school was saved, but the trauma lingered. Daniel became a hero, though many still questioned the source of his information.

The following days were a blur of interviews and questions. Daniel's mother hugged him tightly, her eyes filled with tears. "I'm so proud of you," she said. "You saved so many lives."

Daniel felt a mix of relief and exhaustion. He had done what he set out to do, but the weight of the experience weighed heavily on him.

The school was abuzz with talk of the near-tragedy. Students and teachers alike were in shock, trying to process what had almost

Whispers of the Forgotten

happened. Daniel found himself at the center of attention, with many wonderings how he had known.

During one particularly tense moment, the school counselor, Mrs. Garcia, called Daniel into her office. "Daniel, I want to understand how you knew about this. Can you explain it to me?"

Daniel hesitated, knowing that the truth might be too much for her to handle. "I just had a feeling," he said finally. "I saw the signs."

Mrs. Garcia looked at him, her eyes filled with concern. "If you ever need to talk about anything, my door is always open."

Daniel nodded, grateful for her understanding. But he knew he couldn't share the whole truth. Not yet.

That evening, as Daniel sat in his room, Emily and Samuel appeared once more. "You did well, Daniel," Samuel said. "But there are still many questions that need answers."

Daniel felt a sense of unease. "What do you mean?"

"There are darker forces at play," Samuel continued. "Forces that know you can see them. You must be careful."

Emily nodded; her eyes filled with worry. "We're here to help you, but you need to stay vigilant."

Daniel felt a chill run down his spine. He knew that the danger was far from over.

Chapter 12
<u>Unanswered Questions</u>

Despite the success, Daniel couldn't shake the feeling that something was left unresolved. The ghosts grew restless, their whispers more urgent. Emily appeared one final time, her face etched with worry.

"Daniel, this isn't over," she said. "There are darker forces at play. They know you can see them. Be careful."

As Emily faded away, Daniel felt a chill run down his spine. The real horror was just beginning.

Determined to uncover the truth, Daniel continued to seek guidance from the spirits. He also spent more time with Ethan and Mrs. Thompson, hoping to piece together the larger puzzle.

Whispers of the Forgotten

One evening, while exploring the attic, Daniel discovered an old photograph of his grandfather with a group of people. On the back, a note read: "The Society of Light – 1952."

Curious, Daniel showed the photo to Mrs. Thompson. Her eyes widened with recognition. "The Society of Light was a group dedicated to studying and combating supernatural forces," she explained. "Your grandfather was a founding member."

Daniel felt a surge of pride and determination. "I need to learn more about them. Maybe they have answers."

With Mrs. Thompson's help, Daniel delved into the history of the Society of Light. They discovered records of their battles against dark entities and their efforts to protect the living from malevolent spirits.

As Daniel read through the documents, he felt a sense of connection to his grandfather. He realized that his gift – his curse – was part of a larger legacy.

One night, as Daniel sat in his room, he felt a cold breeze and saw a figure standing in the corner. It was a woman, her eyes filled with sorrow.

"Who are you?" Daniel asked, his voice trembling.

"I am Sarah," the woman replied. "I was a victim of violence many years ago. I have come to help you."

Daniel felt a wave of compassion for her. "Thank you, Sarah. We need all the help we can get."

Sarah nodded. "I will guide you. You must trust your instincts and act quickly."

With Sarah's guidance, Daniel felt a renewed sense of determination. He and his friends continued to refine their plan, ensuring they were ready for whatever might happen.

As the day of the shooting approached, Daniel and his friends grew more anxious. They double-checked their plans, ensuring everything was in place. The ghosts continued to provide guidance, their whispers growing more urgent.

Daniel tried one last time to warn his mother. "Mom, please, you have to believe me. Something terrible is going to happen."

Anna looked at him, her expression pained. "Daniel, I love you, but I can't take action based on visions. Please, try to stay calm."

Daniel felt a surge of frustration, but he knew he couldn't give up. He and Lily had to act, with or without help from the authorities.

With the spirits' guidance, Daniel and his friends positioned themselves strategically around the school, ready to act at a moment's notice. The air was thick with tension, each second dragging on like an eternity.

Chapter 13
<u>The Cliffhanger</u>

Daniel stood at his grandfather's grave, a sense of foreboding washing over him. He had saved his school, but the ghosts' warnings echoed in his mind. The battle against the unseen was far from over, and Daniel knew he had to be ready.

He turned to leave, but the air grew cold, and a shadow fell over the grave. Daniel felt a presence behind him, a dark, malevolent force. He spun around, but there was nothing there.

"Stay vigilant," the ghosts whispered. "The darkness is watching."

Daniel took a deep breath, steeling himself for the challenges ahead. He knew he couldn't let his guard down, not even for a moment.

Whispers of the Forgotten

As he walked away from the grave, Daniel felt a strange sense of resolve. He knew that the road ahead would be difficult, but he was ready to face it. With the support of his friends and the guidance of the spirits, he would confront the darkness and protect those he loved.

That night, as Daniel sat in his room, he felt a cold breeze and saw a figure standing in the corner. It was a man, his eyes filled with malice.

"Who are you?" Daniel asked, his voice trembling.

"I am the darkness," the man replied. "And I am coming for you."

Daniel felt a chill run down his spine. He knew that the real battle was about to begin.

Ethan Shadows

Epilogue

Daniel sat in his room; the journal open before him. He had saved his school, but the journey was far from over. The ghosts had warned him of a greater threat, a darkness that lurked in the shadows.

He knew he had to be prepared, to learn more about his gift – his curse. With the support of his friends and the guidance of the spirits, he would face whatever came next.

The battle against the unseen had only just begun.

As he closed the journal, Daniel felt a sense of determination. He knew that he couldn't let his guard down. The darkness was watching, and he had to be ready.

With a deep breath, Daniel stood up and looked out the window. The night was dark and still, but he knew that he wasn't alone.

Whispers of the Forgotten

Ethan Shadows

The spirits were with him, guiding him, protecting him.

The road ahead would be difficult, but Daniel was ready to face it. With his friends by his side and the spirits to guide him, he would confront the darkness and protect those he loved.

The battle had only just begun.

Ethan Shadows

Whispers of the Forgotten